The Legend of
Sleepy Hollow

Copyright © 1991 by Ideals Publishing Corporation

All rights reserved. No part of this publication may be
reproduced or transmitted in any form or by any means,
electronic or mechanical, including photocopy, recording,
or any information storage and retrieval system, without
permission in writing from the publisher.

Published by Ideals Publishing Corporation
Nashville, Tennessee 37210

Printed and bound in the United States of America

ISBN 0-8249-8162-6

Library of Congress Card Catalog # 91-072020
Library of Congress Cataloging-in-Publication Data is available.

The illustrations in this book were rendered in oil paints.
The text type was set in New Baskerville.
The display type was set in Antique Caslon.
Color separations were made by Rayson Films, Inc.,
Waukesha, Wisconsin.
Printed and bound by Arcata Graphics Kingsport,
Kingsport, Tennessee.

THE LEGEND OF
SLEEPY HOLLOW

Adapted from the original by
Washington Irving

Illustrated by
Russ Flint

Ideals Children's Books • Nashville, Tennessee

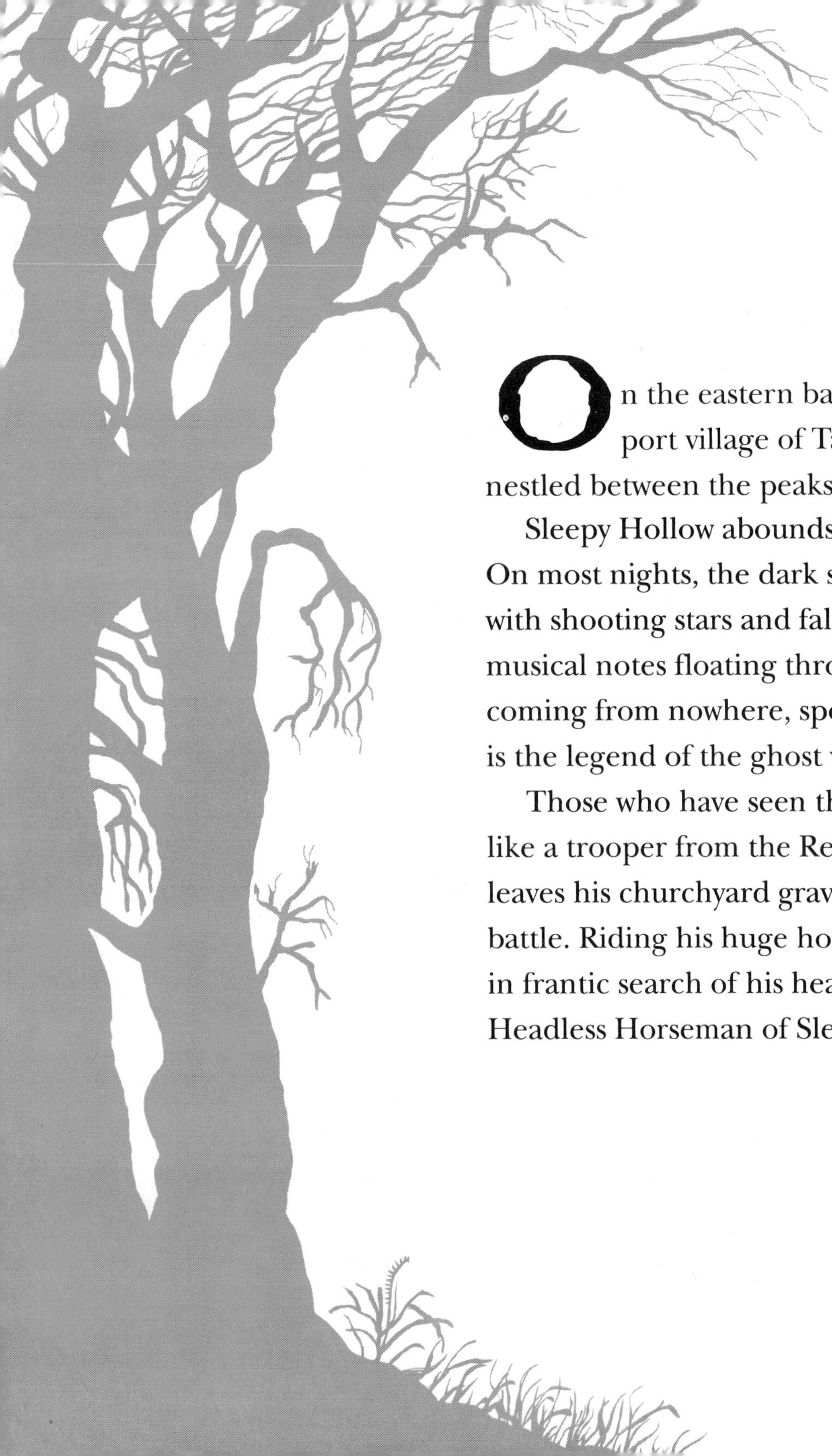

On the eastern bank of the lazy Tappan Zee River lies the little port village of Tarry Town. Over the closest mountain, nestled between the peaks, rests the small valley of Sleepy Hollow.

Sleepy Hollow abounds with strange and wonderful happenings. On most nights, the dark skies of the sleeping community are ablaze with shooting stars and falling meteors. The inhabitants tell of odd musical notes floating through the air and of voices whispering, coming from nowhere, spoken by no one. Most remarkable, however, is the legend of the ghost who haunts the region.

Those who have seen the ghost say he wears a long, woolen cape, like a trooper from the Revolutionary War. Each night, the ghost leaves his churchyard grave and hurries to the site of a long-forgotten battle. Riding his huge horse like the midnight fury, he is a body in frantic search of his head—lost in some raging battle. He is the Headless Horseman of Sleepy Hollow!

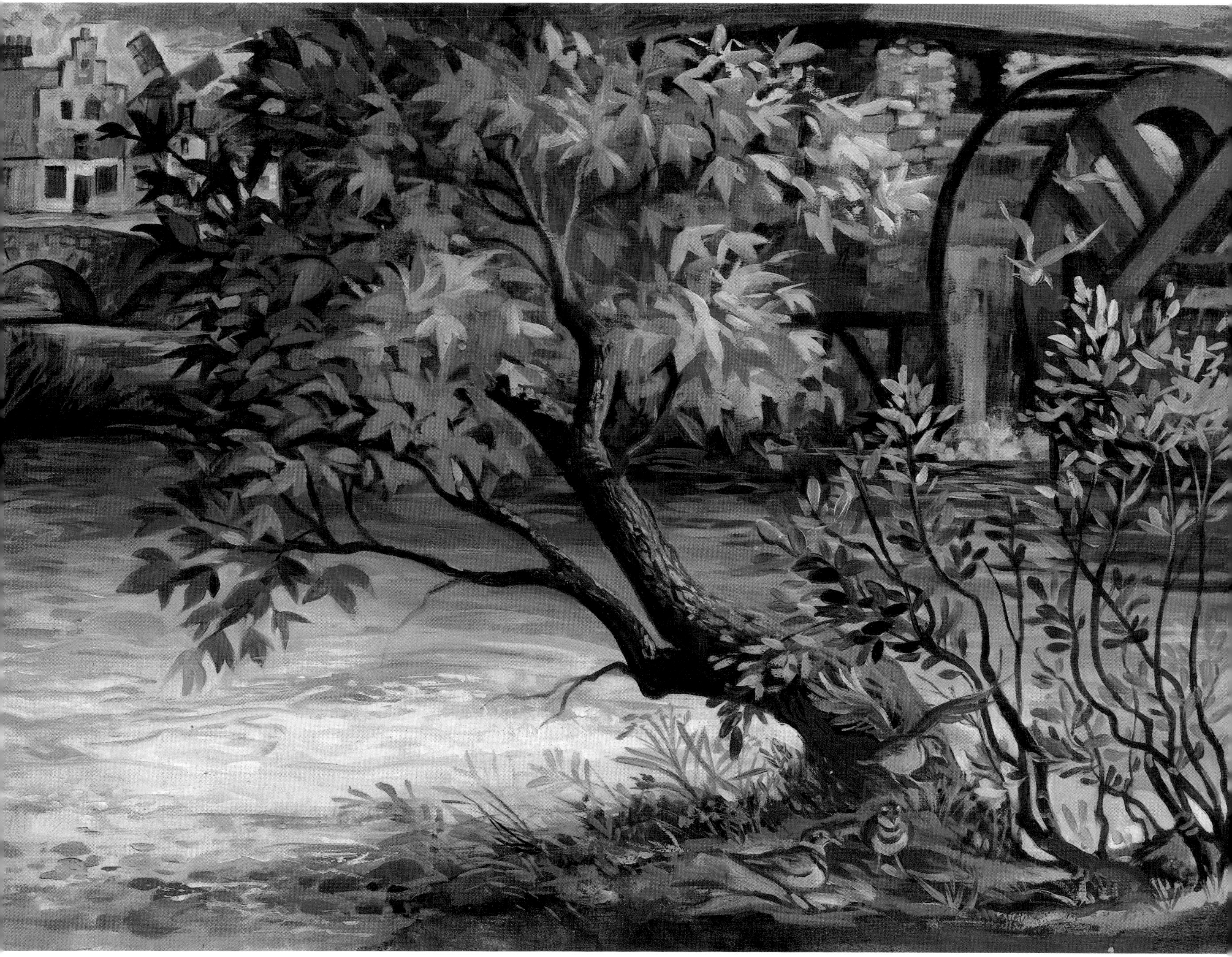

Into this sleepy little community came a new schoolmaster named Ichabod Crane. Aptly named, he was tall and thin, with long skinny arms and legs. With one leg tucked up under his body, he could have been mistaken for a crane or a heron. His hands dangled far below his sleeves, and his feet were big enough to serve as shovels. His large eyes darted about in his tiny head, and his ears stuck out on both sides.

The schoolmaster was not mean, but he firmly believed in the saying, "Spare the rod and spoil the child." The large birch trees growing just outside the schoolhouse door provided handy branches which Ichabod applied to the legs and hands of tardy or disobedient pupils.

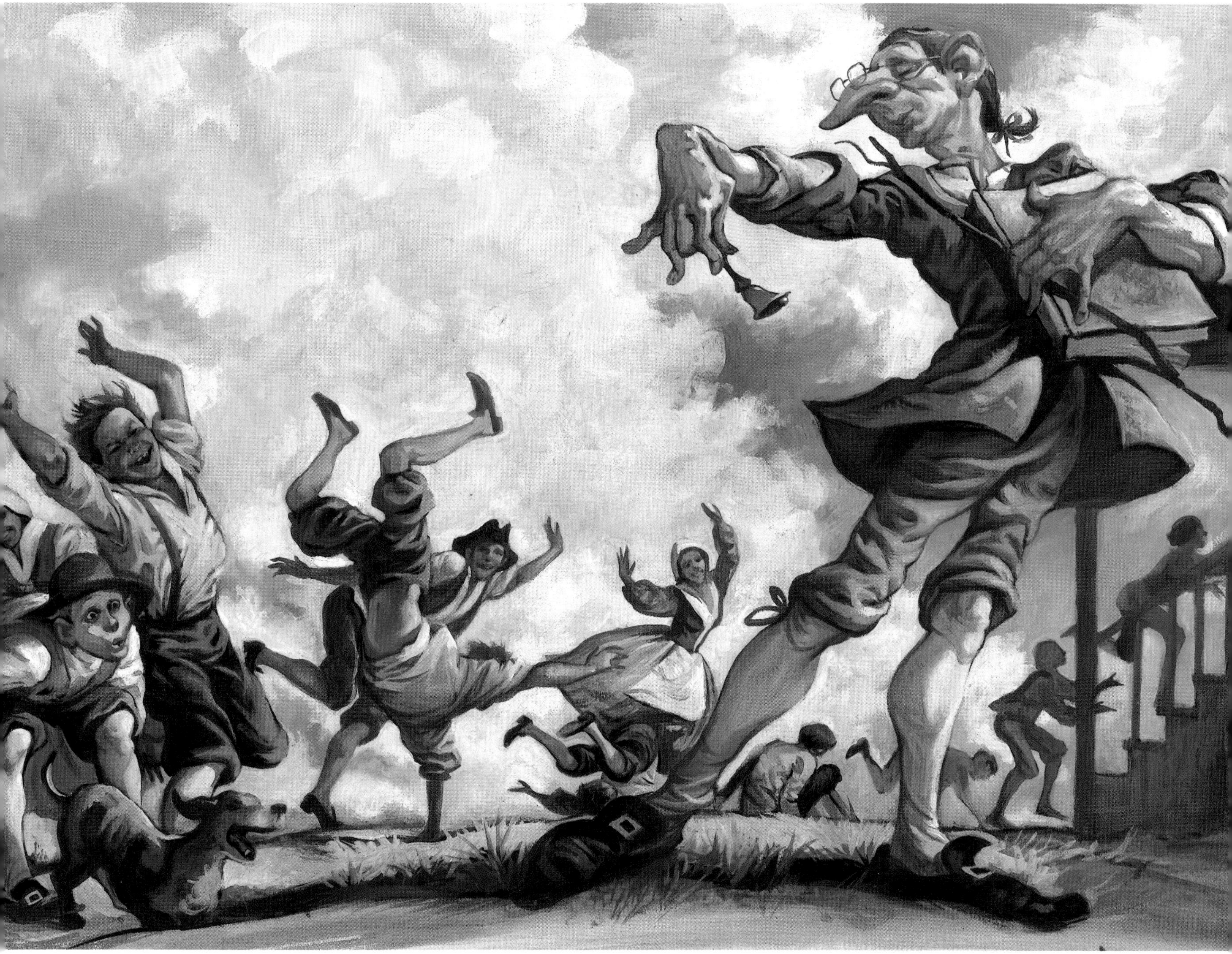

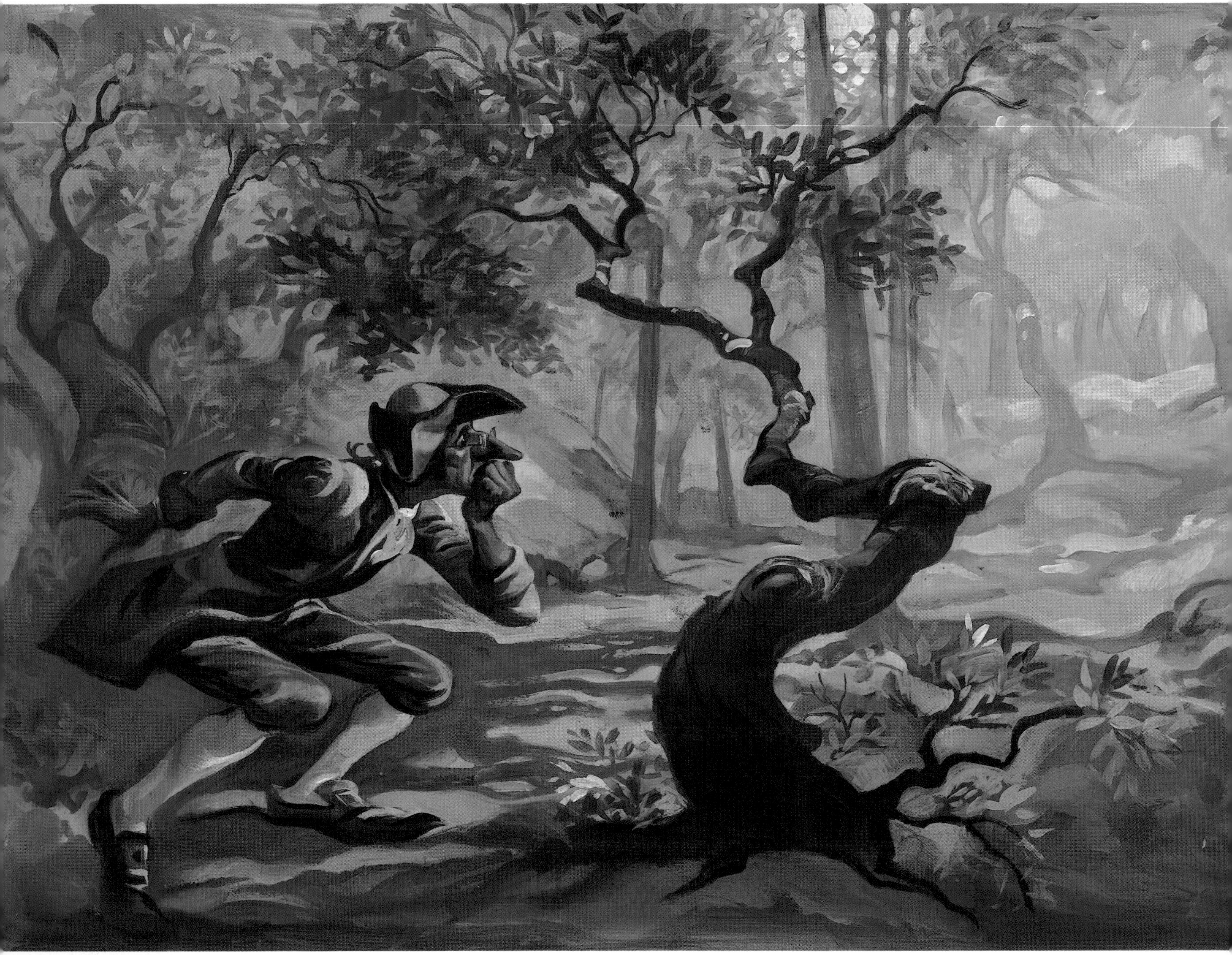

Ichabod made little money for his services, so local parents took turns letting the schoolmaster live with them. Ichabod stayed one week at the home of one pupil, and moved to the home of another the following week. To earn extra money, he gave singing lessons to the young ladies of the community. He often had dinner with these pupils.

Over supper Ichabod told his hosts all the local gossip he heard. After dessert, he and the women gathered around the fireplace to exchange tales of ghosts and witchcraft. They told marvelous tales of haunted fields and brooks and bridges, and, in particular, they told tales of the Headless Horseman.

The excitement of the stories, however, turned into terrifying memories during the long walk home. Ichabod trembled at dark shadows and unrecognizable shapes. Shadows would cast long, headless forms on the path, and he would freeze, listening for galloping hooves. Then, realizing it was only the wind in the trees and not the Headless Horseman, Ichabod would continue on his way, walking much faster the rest of the way to his temporary bed.

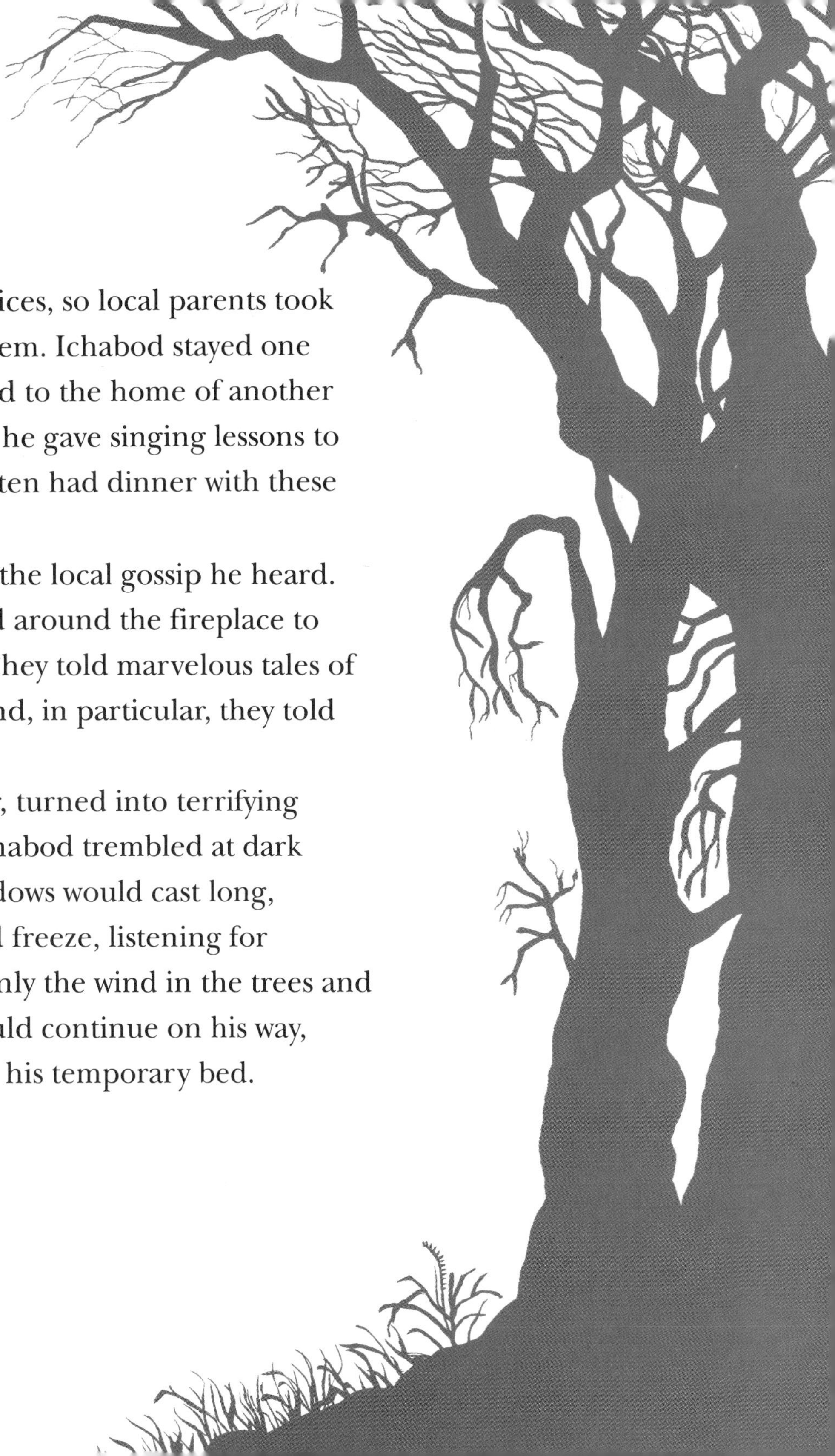

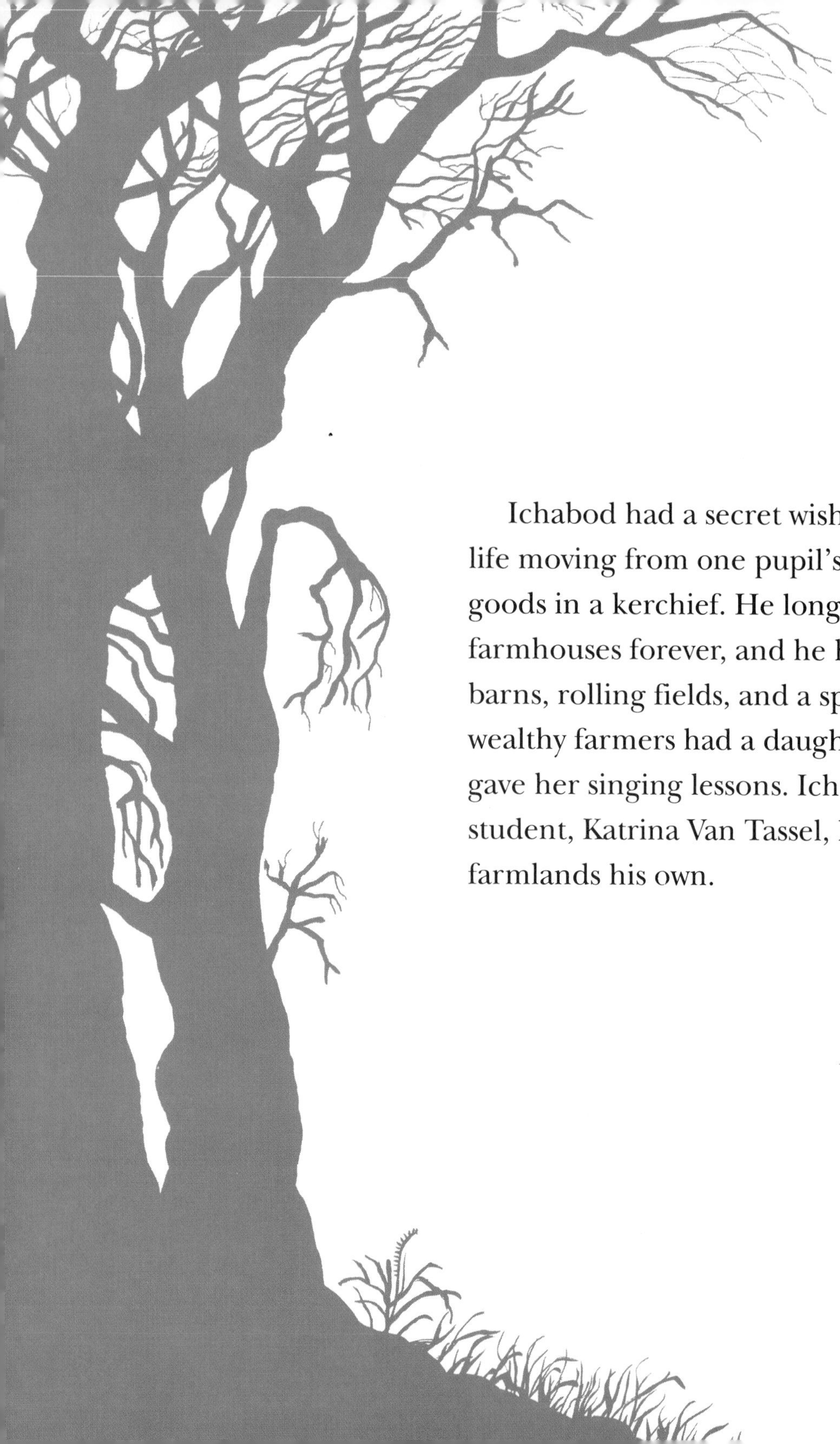

Ichabod had a secret wish. He did not want to spend the rest of his life moving from one pupil's house to another, carrying all his worldly goods in a kerchief. He longed to live in one of the valley's huge farmhouses forever, and he hoped to marry into a family with large barns, rolling fields, and a sprawling home. One of Sleepy Hollow's wealthy farmers had a daughter who was not yet married, and Ichabod gave her singing lessons. Ichabod was determined to make this student, Katrina Van Tassel, his wife, and to make her father's farmlands his own.

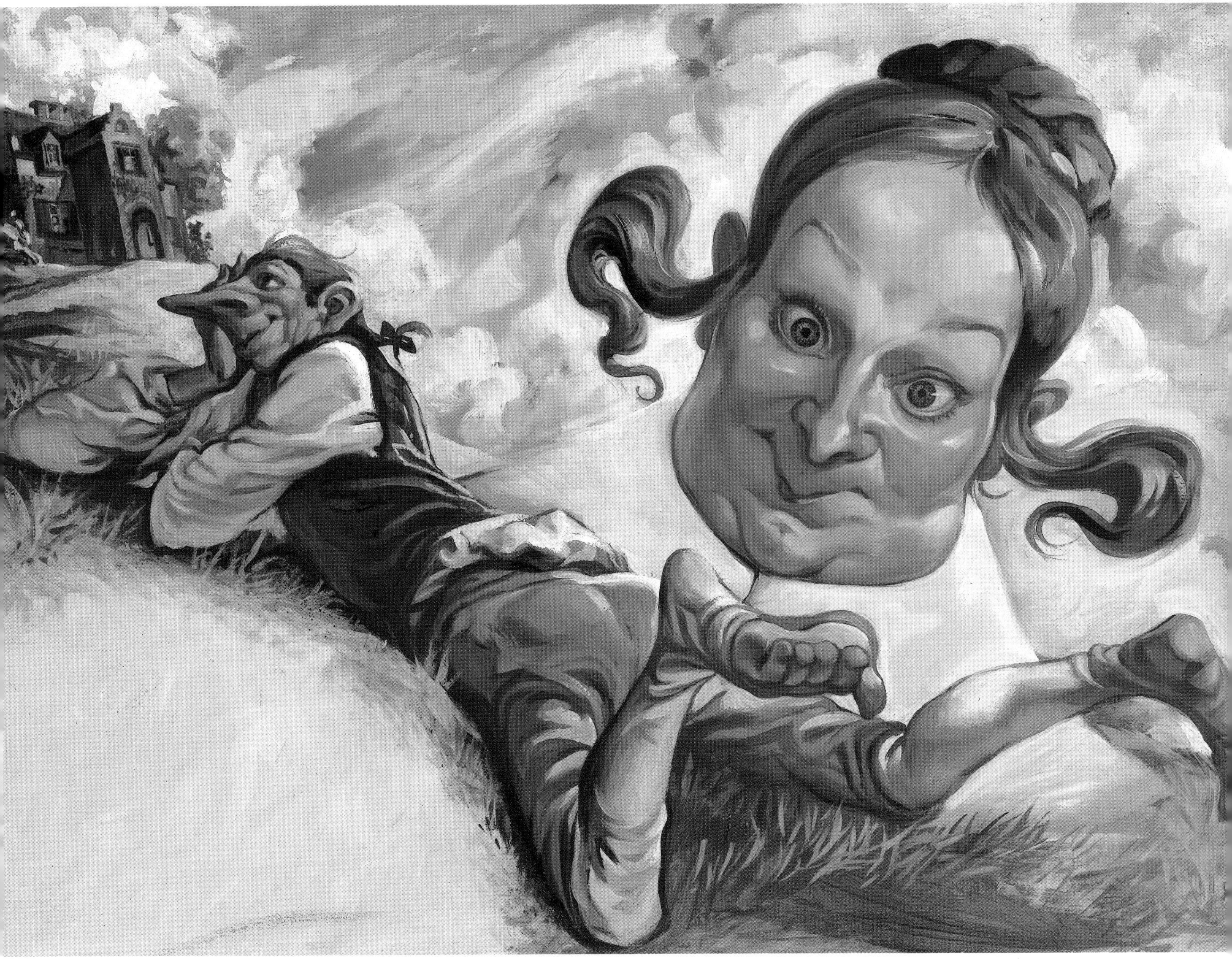

Unfortunately for Ichabod, Katrina already had a suitor. He was tall, with a huge chest and muscular arms. His name was Brom Van Brunt, but, because of his great strength, his friends called him Brom Bones.

Boasting that he was the strongest man in the county, Brom entered every horse race, and he and his horse, Daredevil, always won. Everybody loved Brom, and he loved practical jokes and pranks. When the local folks awoke at midnight and heard horses galloping past their farmhouses, they smiled at the whooping and hollering and exclaimed, "There goes Brom Bones and his gang!"

A silent feud arose between Brom and the schoolmaster as they competed to win Katrina's hand. Ichabod tried to impress Katrina with his knowledge of books and with his singing, while Brom, at every opportunity, tried to embarrass Ichabod.

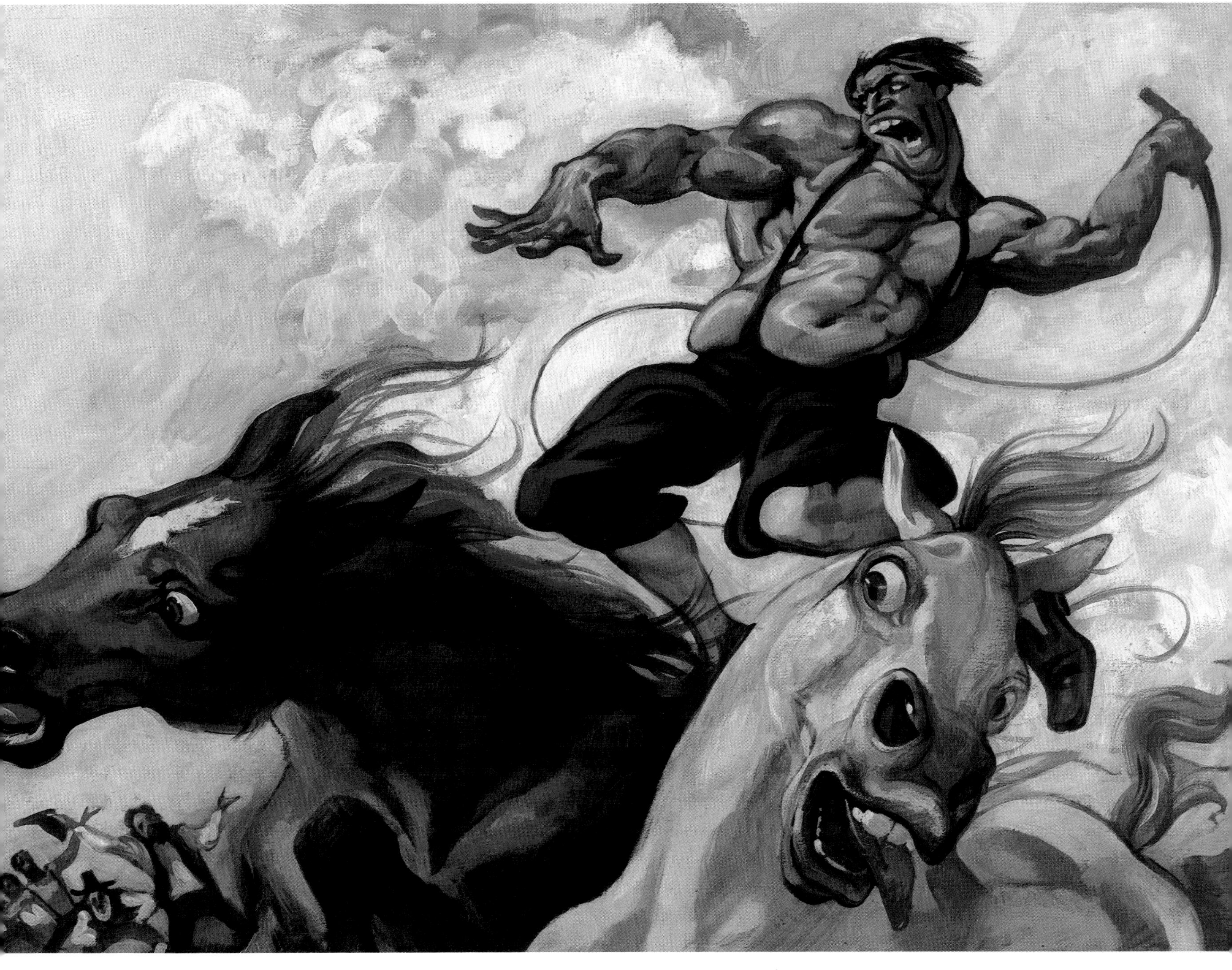

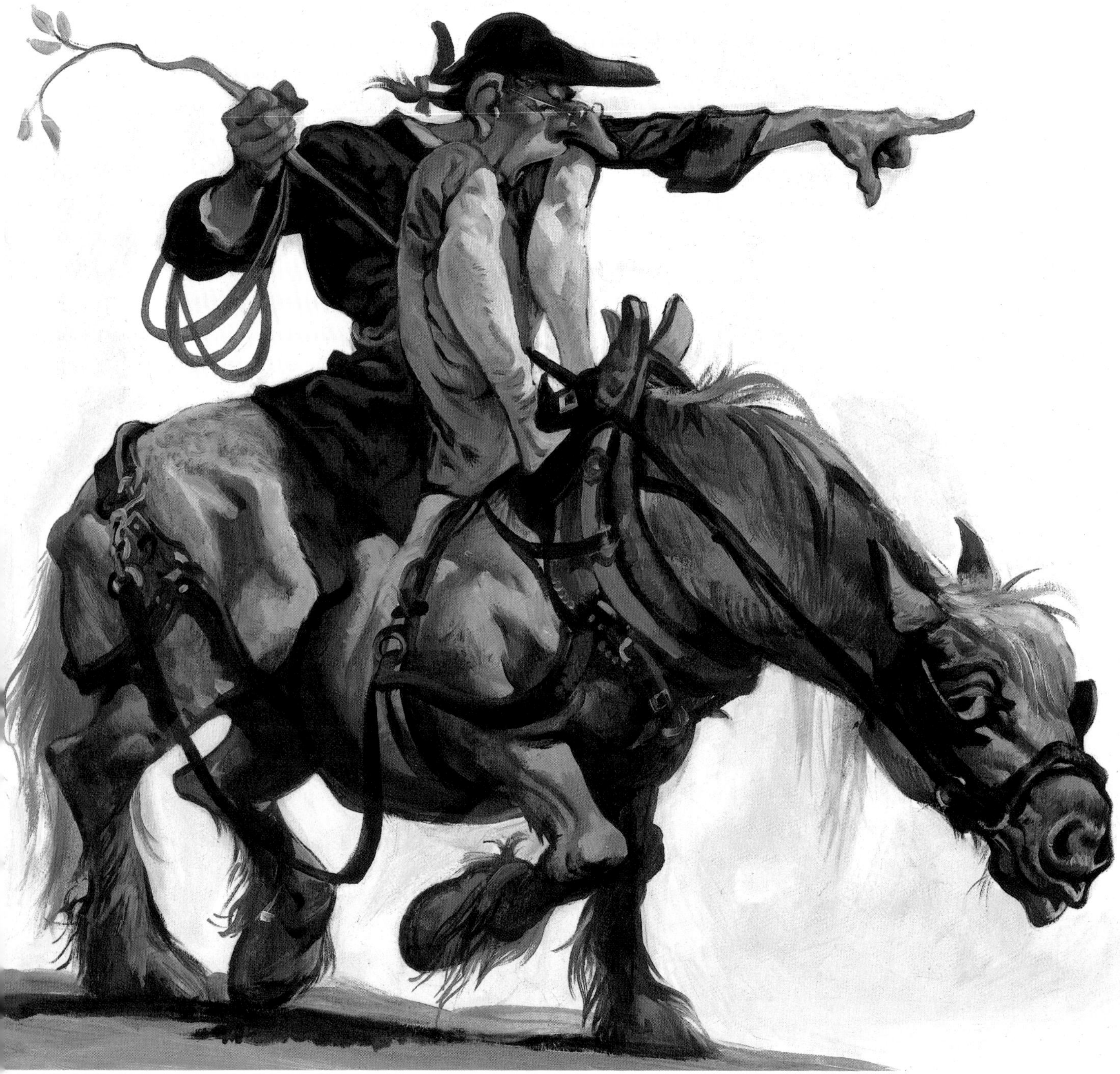

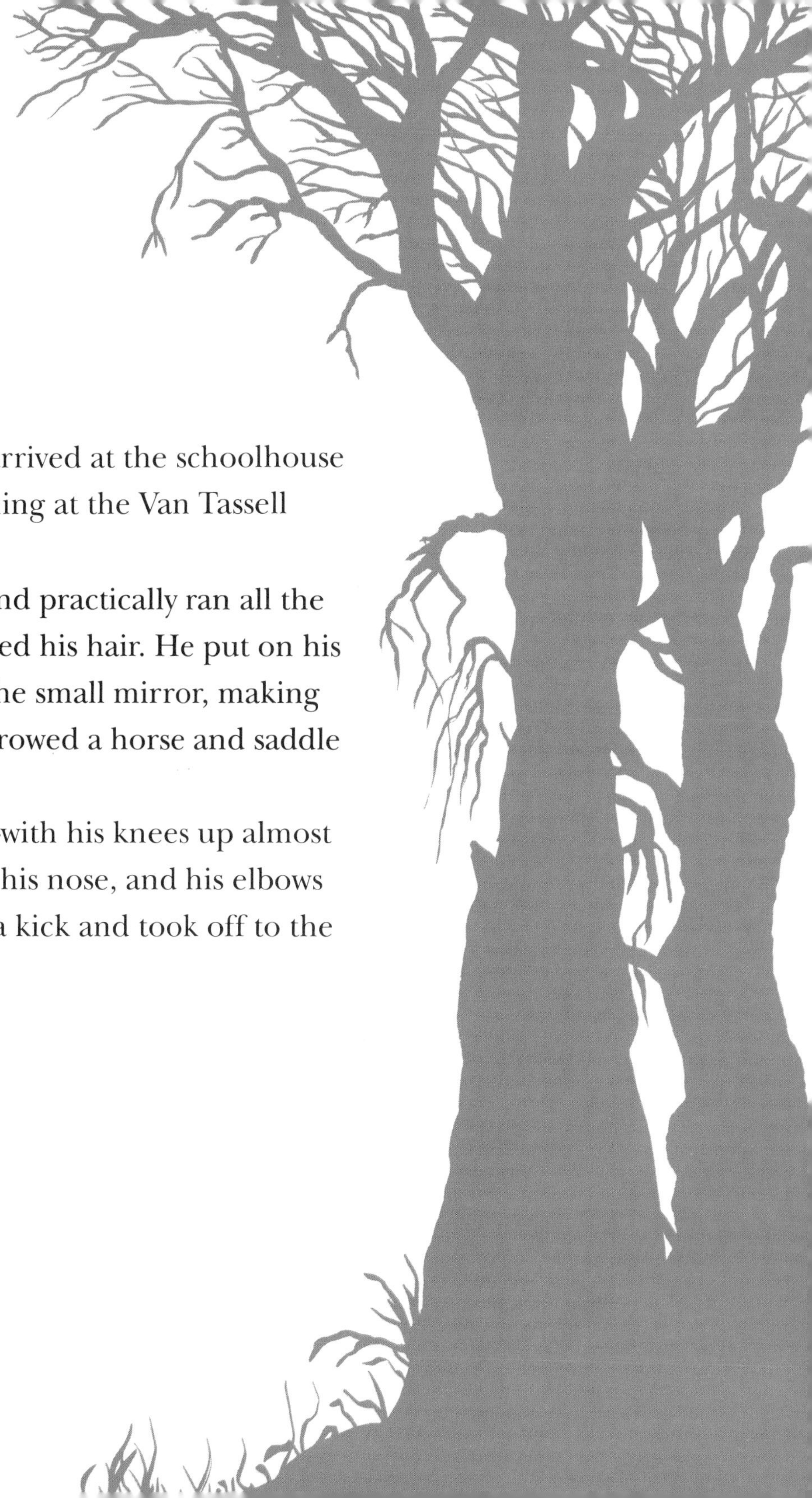

On one sunny autumn day, a messenger arrived at the schoolhouse and invited Ichabod to a party that very evening at the Van Tassell farmhouse.

Ichabod dismissed school an hour early and practically ran all the way home. He shaved and washed and combed his hair. He put on his only suit and inspected himself carefully in the small mirror, making certain he looked his very best. Then he borrowed a horse and saddle from his host.

Ichabod mounted Old Gunpowder and—with his knees up almost to his chin, a small woolen hat perched over his nose, and his elbows out like a grasshopper's—he gave the horse a kick and took off to the Van Tassel farm.

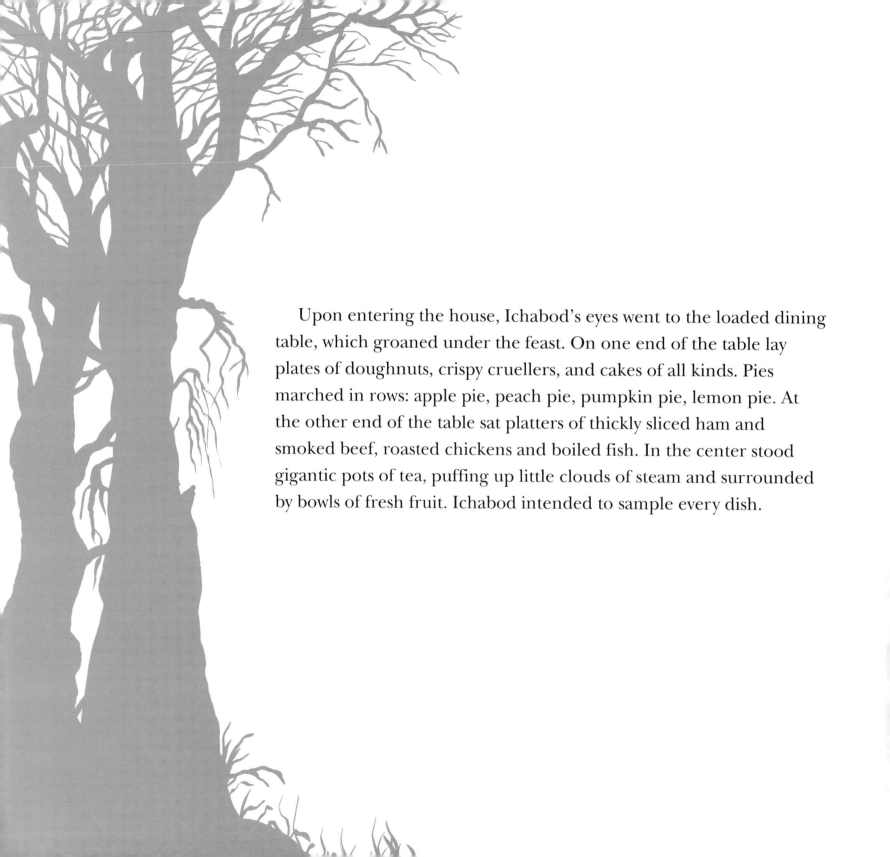

Upon entering the house, Ichabod's eyes went to the loaded dining table, which groaned under the feast. On one end of the table lay plates of doughnuts, crispy cruellers, and cakes of all kinds. Pies marched in rows: apple pie, peach pie, pumpkin pie, lemon pie. At the other end of the table sat platters of thickly sliced ham and smoked beef, roasted chickens and boiled fish. In the center stood gigantic pots of tea, puffing up little clouds of steam and surrounded by bowls of fresh fruit. Ichabod intended to sample every dish.

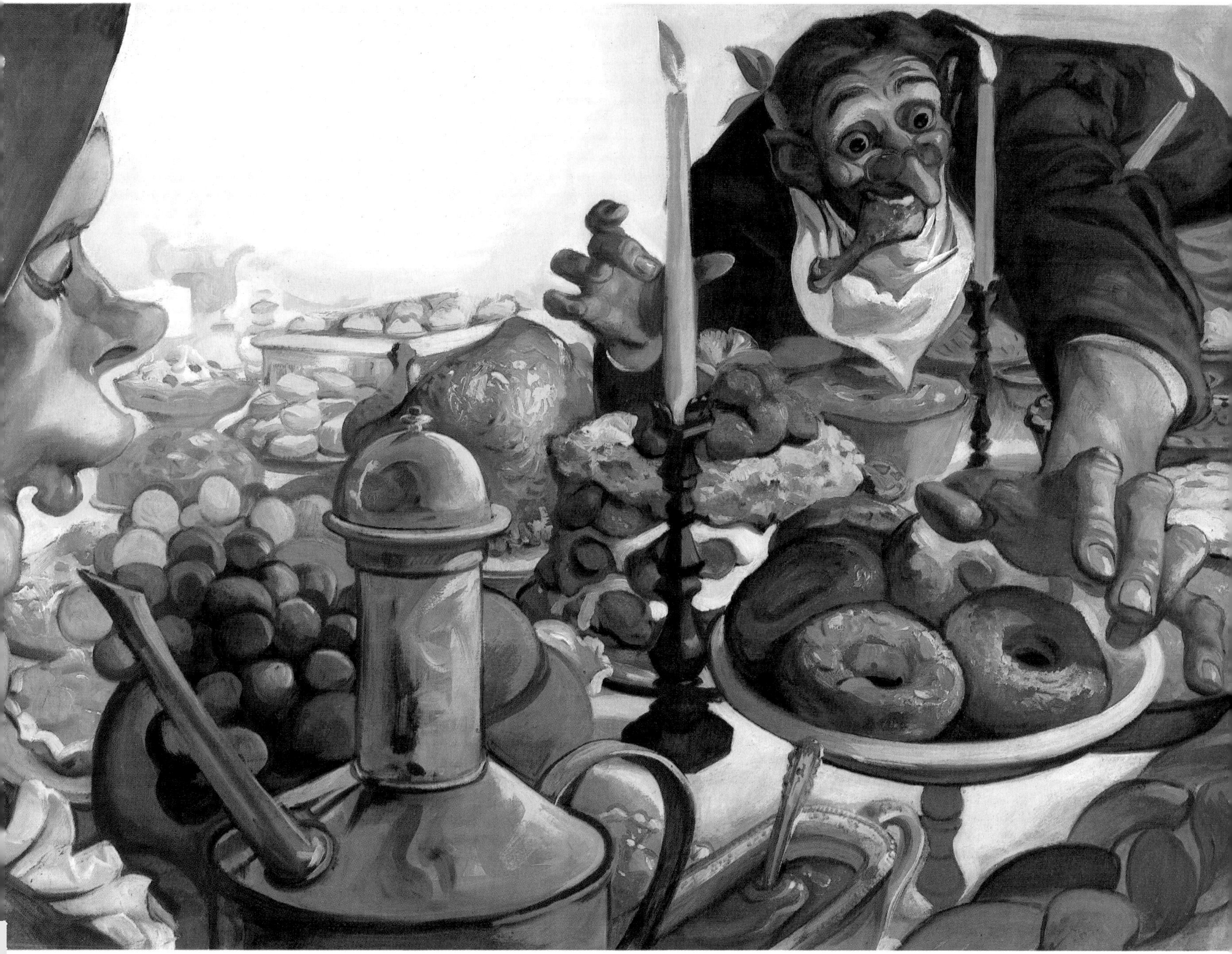

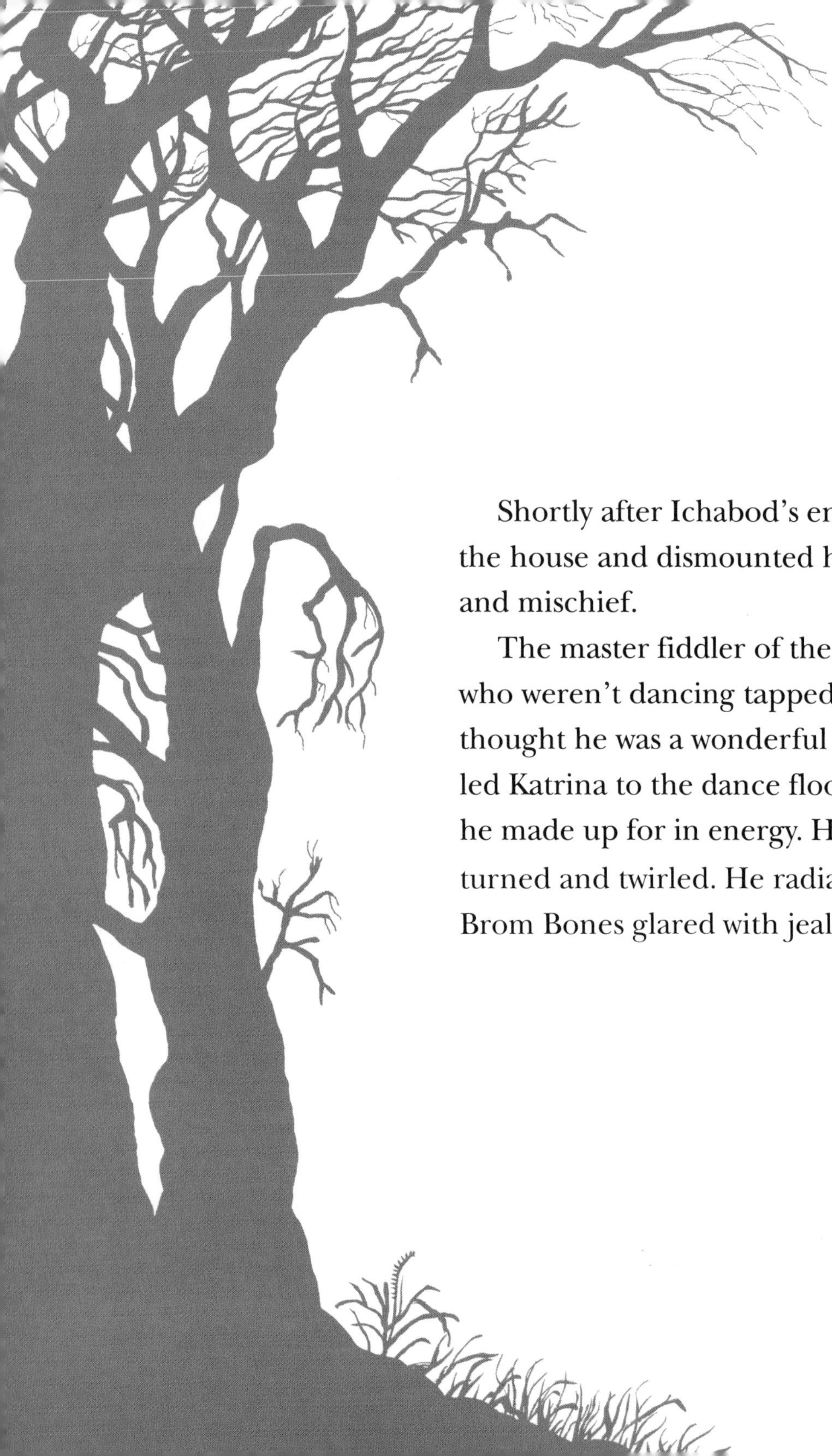

Shortly after Ichabod's entrance, Brom Bones rode up in front of the house and dismounted his favorite horse, Daredevil, full of fire and mischief.

The master fiddler of the county soon started the music. Those who weren't dancing tapped their toes to the fiddler's beat. Ichabod thought he was a wonderful dancer, so as soon as the music began, he led Katrina to the dance floor. What the schoolmaster lacked in grace, he made up for in energy. He bobbed and bounced. He twitched and turned and twirled. He radiated joy. Meanwhile, watching the dancers, Brom Bones glared with jealousy on his face and fire in his eyes.

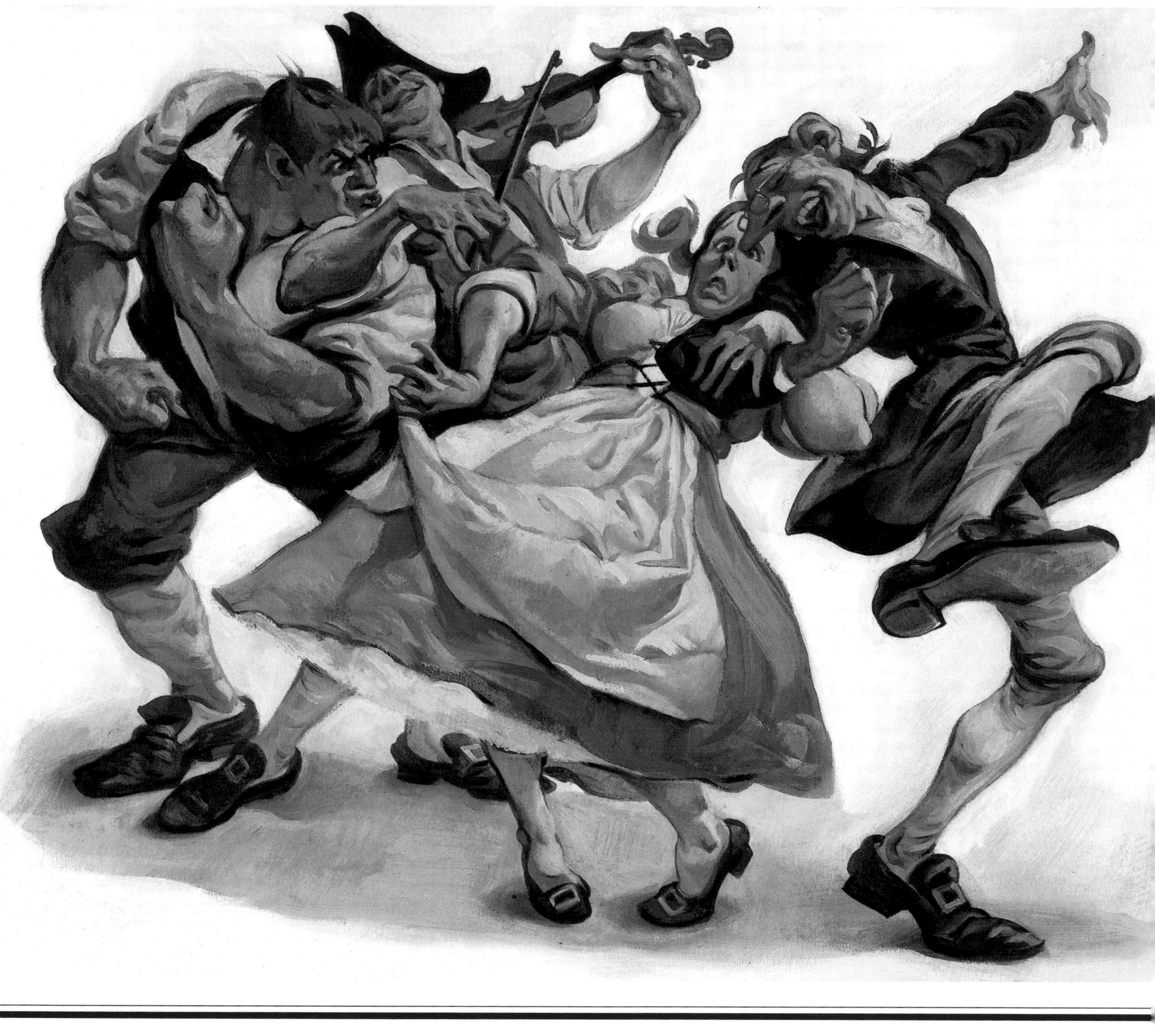

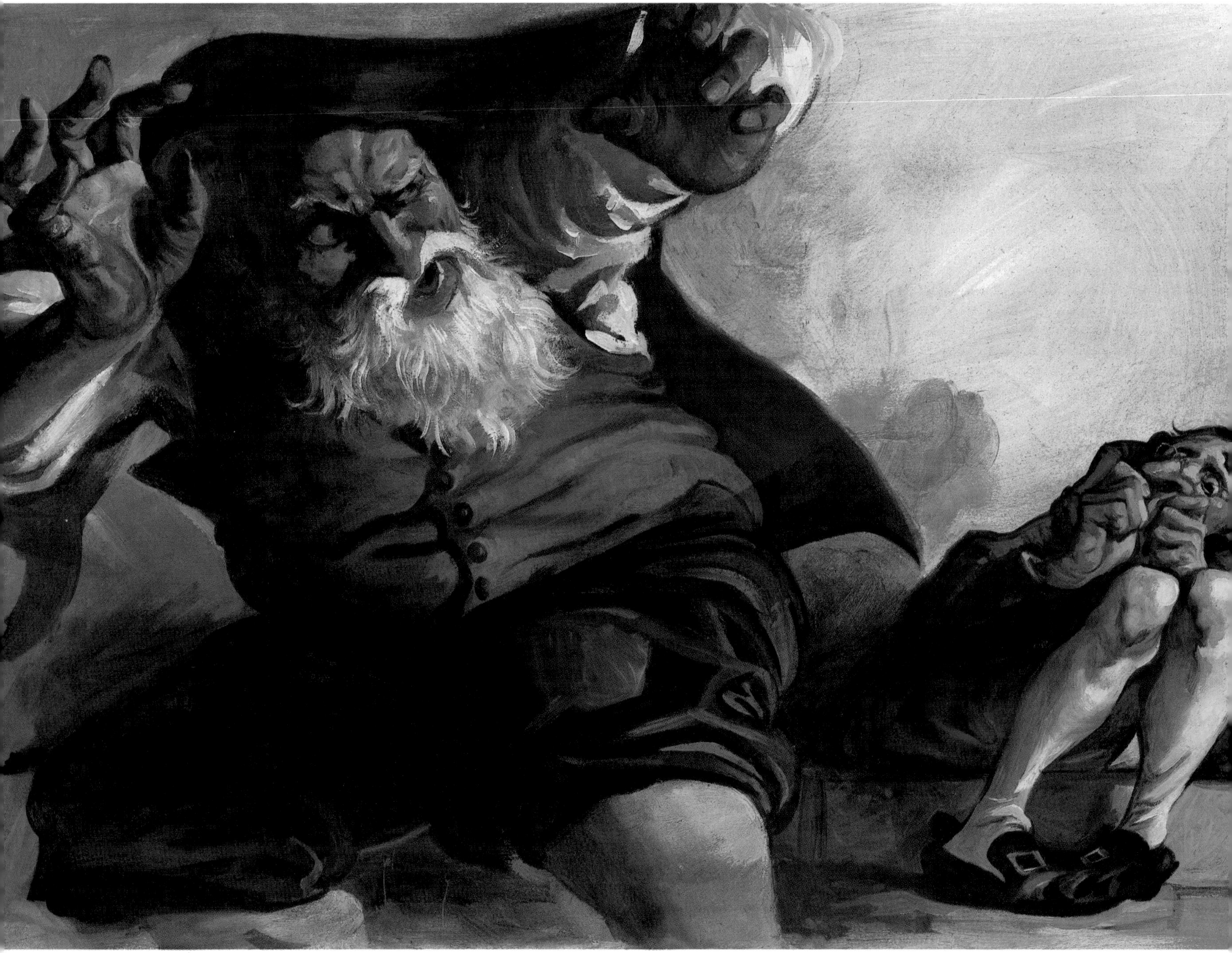

When the music stopped and the dance ended, Ichabod joined a group of people on the porch who were telling stories of the Headless Horseman. Someone said that in the nightly search for his head, the goblin tied up his horse among the graves in the local churchyard.

The church stood on a small hill, where a nearby stream trickled over the road. Across the stream lay a wooden plank bridge, shaded by thick overhanging branches. Local folks agreed that this bridge was where the Headless Horseman was most often met.

One old man told of the night his friend Brouwer met the ghost. The Horseman pulled Brouwer up onto his horse, and they galloped over hill and swamp. When they reached the wooden plank bridge, the ghost turned into a skeleton, and the horse threw old Brouwer into the stream. With a clap of thunder, both the skeleton rider and its horse leaped over the treetops!

Brom Bones joined the group and claimed that one evening he was overtaken by the Horseman, whom he challenged to a race. Brom and Daredevil were winning until the Horseman reached the wooden plank bridge where the headless ghost vanished in a pillar of fire!

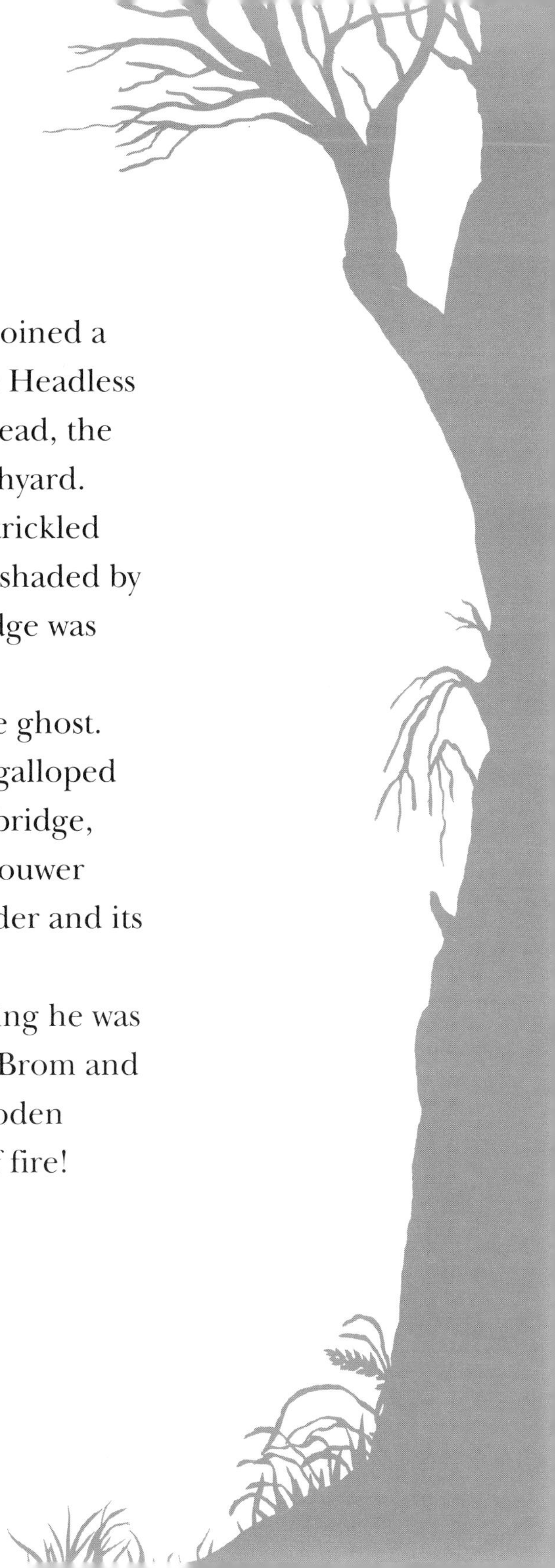

Ichabod listened intently to all these stories until the party broke up. As the farmers loaded their families into their wagons, the schoolmaster lingered behind. Tonight he intended to ask for Katrina's hand. As soon as the other guests left, Ichabod crept up to Katrina's side, put one hand on her arm, and whispered something to her. Startled, she squealed and quickly drew away from Ichabod!

Poor embarrassed Ichabod turned red, scowled, and stomped out of the house. Without looking to the left or right, he headed straight for the stable. With a kick to the horse and a yank on the bridle, he spurred Gunpowder to action.

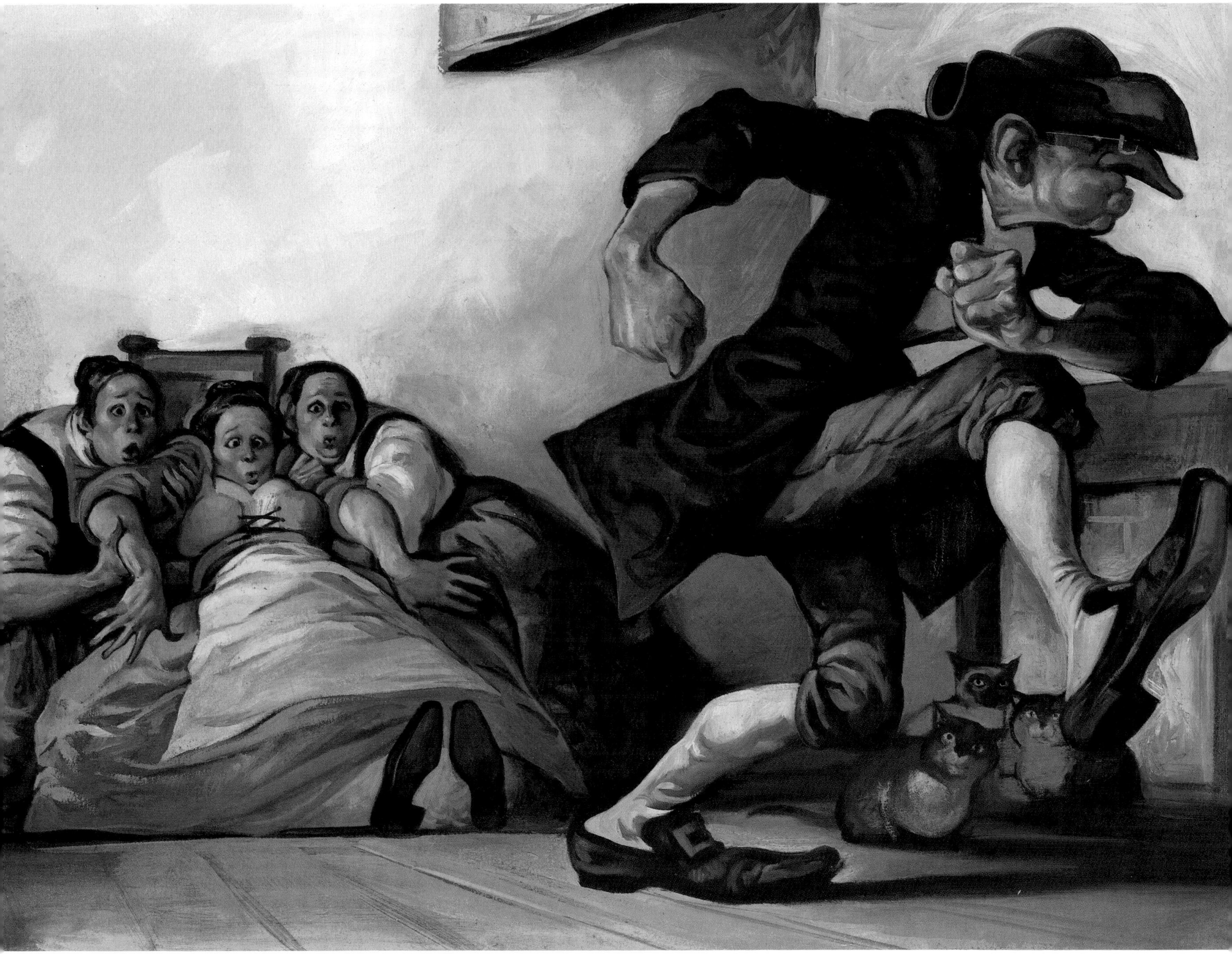

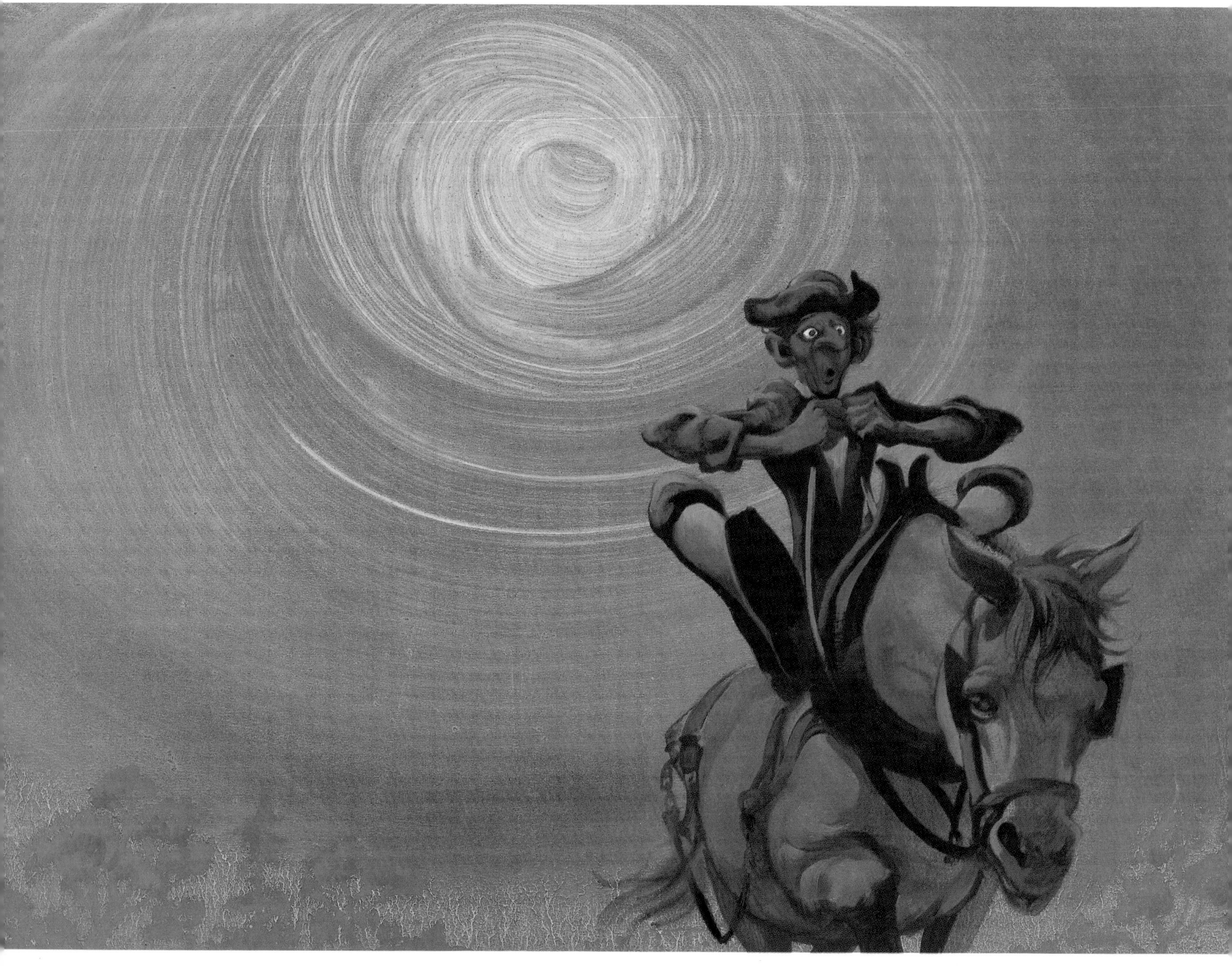

It was past midnight as Ichabod traveled the same roads he so cheerfully had ridden only a few short hours before. The quiet night grew darker as the stars sank back into the sky. Ichabod had never felt so lonely. As he thought of the evening's events, all the scary stories and ghostly tales began to return.

Ichabod nervously began to whistle. He stopped, thinking he heard a whistle in return—but it was only the wind rushing through the trees. He heard a groan—but it was only two branches rubbing against each other. The schoolmaster began to sing.

Up ahead on the road flowed a stream with a few logs laid across as a bridge. On the other side of the bridge, the forest loomed thick with oak and chestnut trees matted with wild vines.

As Ichabod approached the stream, his heart began to thump. He kicked his horse for the dash across, but Old Gunpowder came to a sudden stop. Out of the shadows, there rose a huge, dark figure. It did not move.

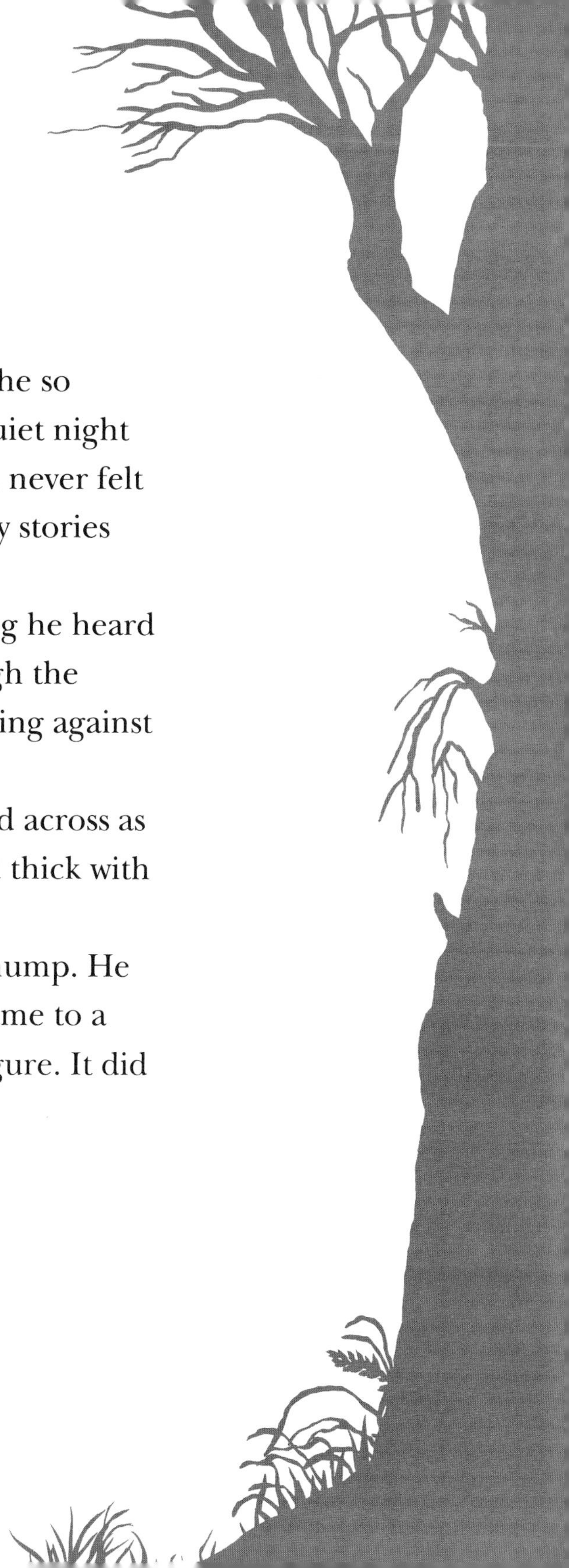

"Who, who are you?" Ichabod stammered.

Instead of answering, the shadowy figure slowly moved to the middle of the road. Ichabod peered into the darkness ahead. He could just make out the form of a large horse upon which towered a huge man covered with a dark flowing cloak.

Ichabod kicked Gunpowder and dashed forward, but the stranger stayed right behind him. Ichabod slowed his horse to a walk and the rider slowed also. Ichabod tried to sing, but his dry tongue clung to the roof of his mouth.

As the pair topped a hill, the silhouette of Ichabod's companion appeared clearly against the sky. Ichabod's eyes flew open in horror! His companion had no head! And the head which should have rested on the horseman's shoulders instead rested on his saddle!

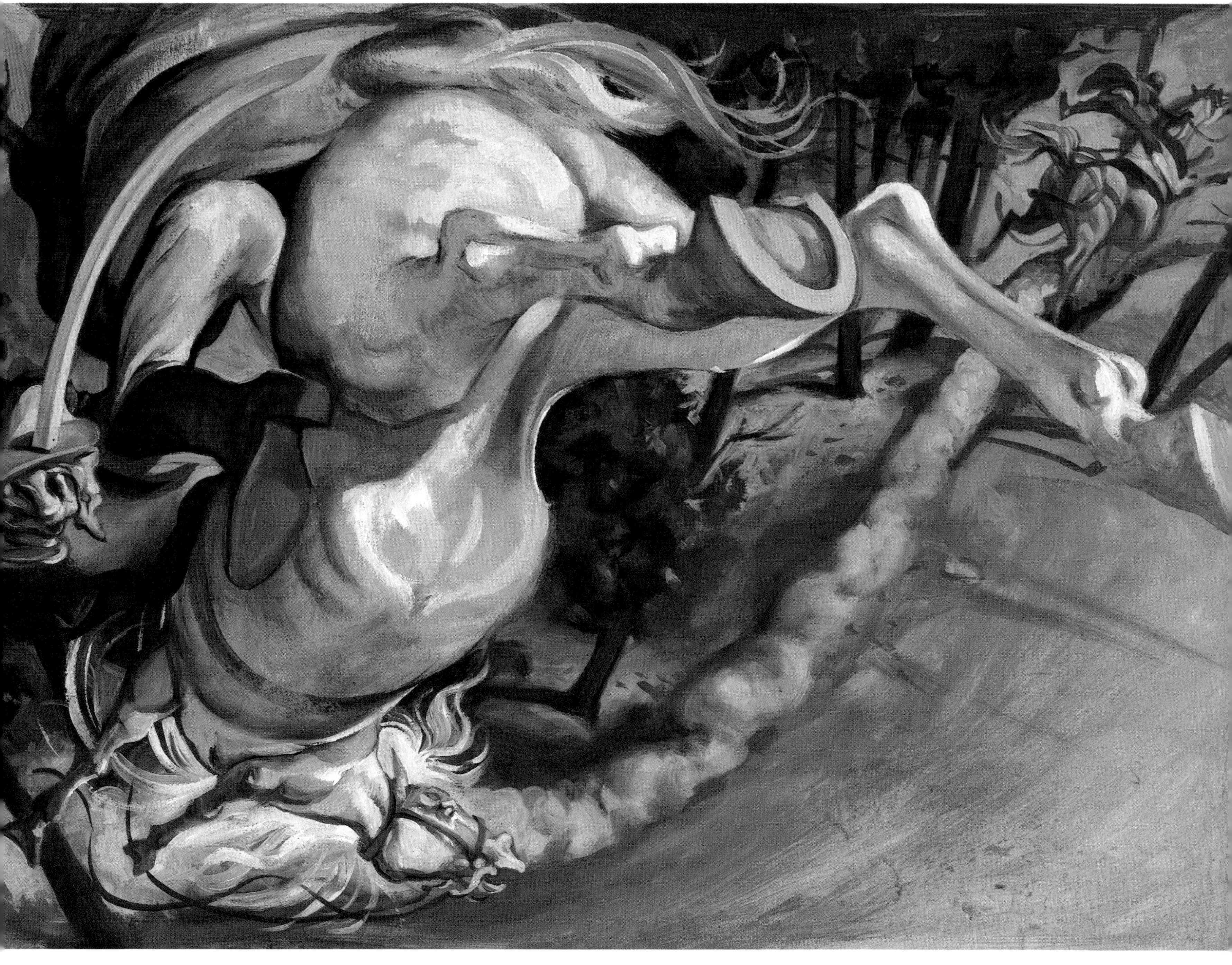

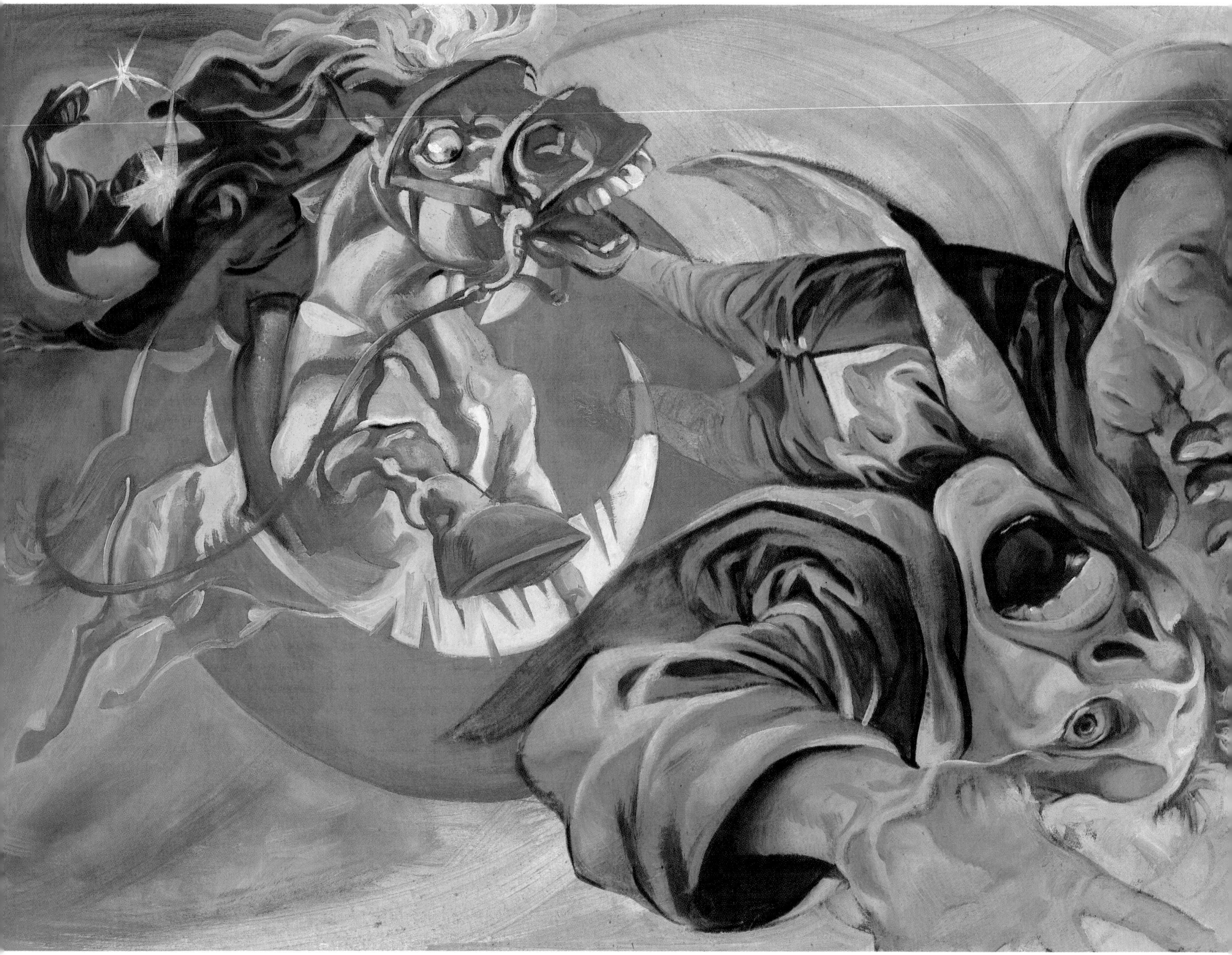

Ichabod kicked and whipped and yelled at Gunpowder. Away they dashed, the ghost matching stride for stride. Stones flew! Sparks flashed! Ichabod's coat fluttered as he stretched over the horse's head.

The riders now approached the road to Sleepy Hollow, but Gunpowder, as if possessed by a devil, bolted toward the opposite road. This road led across the wooden plank bridge and up the hill to the church with its graveyard.

Filled with panic, Ichabod suddenly felt his saddle slipping off. He grabbed Gunpowder around the neck as the saddle slipped to the ground and the ghostly horse trampled it into the dust.

Ahead, through the trees, Ichabod could see the church. He felt the ghost getting closer and heard approaching hoofbeats. Another kick in the ribs and Gunpowder pounded over the bridge. Ichabod turned around, expecting the ghost to disappear. Instead, the goblin stood up in his stirrups and hurled his head at Ichabod!

The schoolmaster tried to dodge the missile but was hit and fell to the ground. Then the ghostly rider and horses thundered past like a whirlwind.

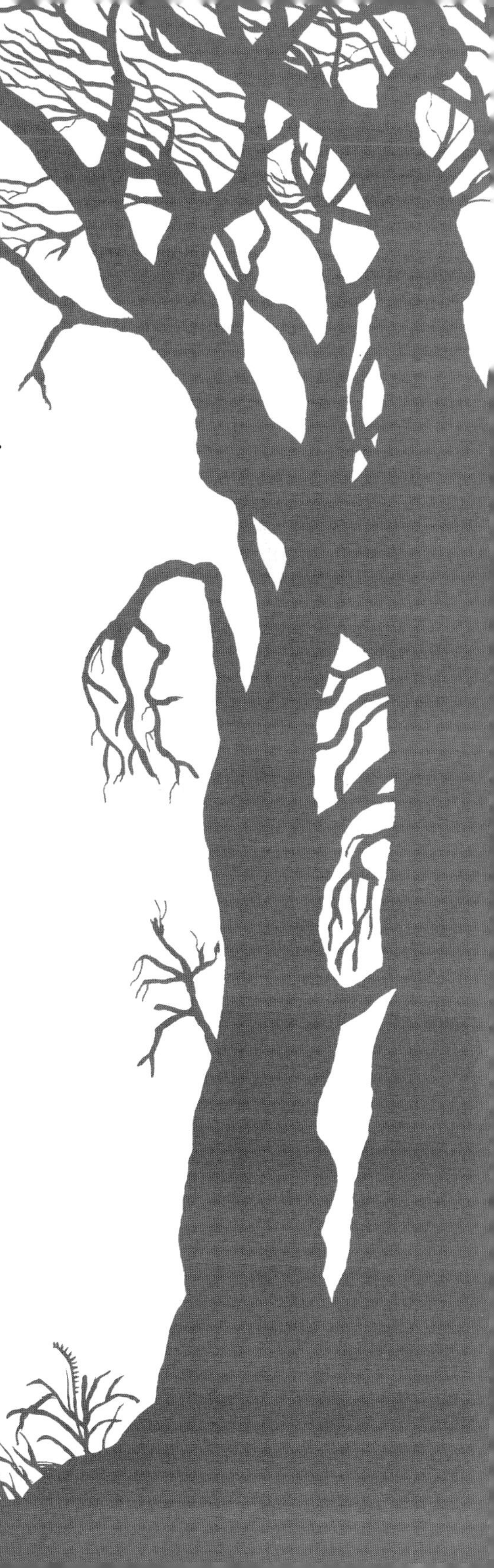

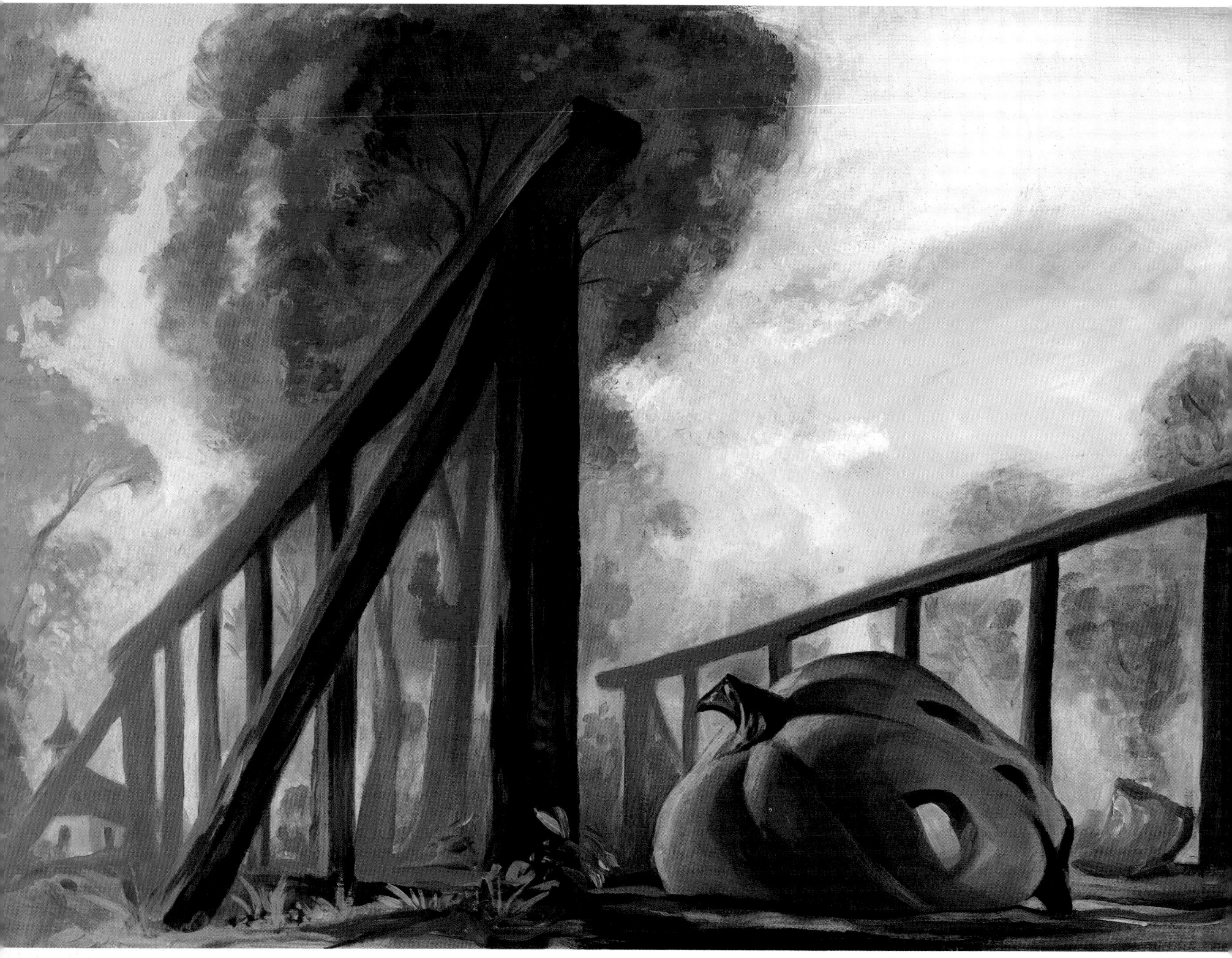

Sunrise found Gunpowder, without saddle or bridle, calmly chomping the grass outside his master's gate. Ichabod could not be found. He did not come to school. He did not appear for dinner.

After searching the area, local folks found the trampled saddle on the road leading to the church. Beyond the bridge, they found Ichabod's hat, and close by they found a shattered pumpkin.

Years later, gossipers said the schoolmaster had left Sleepy Hollow because he was terrified of the ghost and he was embarrassed about losing his sweetheart. Katrina married Brom Bones, who always burst into a hearty laugh at the mention of the pumpkin, and some people believed he knew more than he was telling.

But the old country wives, who know about such things, believe the schoolmaster was spirited away by supernatural means. And those who pass the bridge on a warm summer evening often fancy they hear the voice of the schoolmaster singing a melancholy tune amid the quiet breezes of Sleepy Hollow.

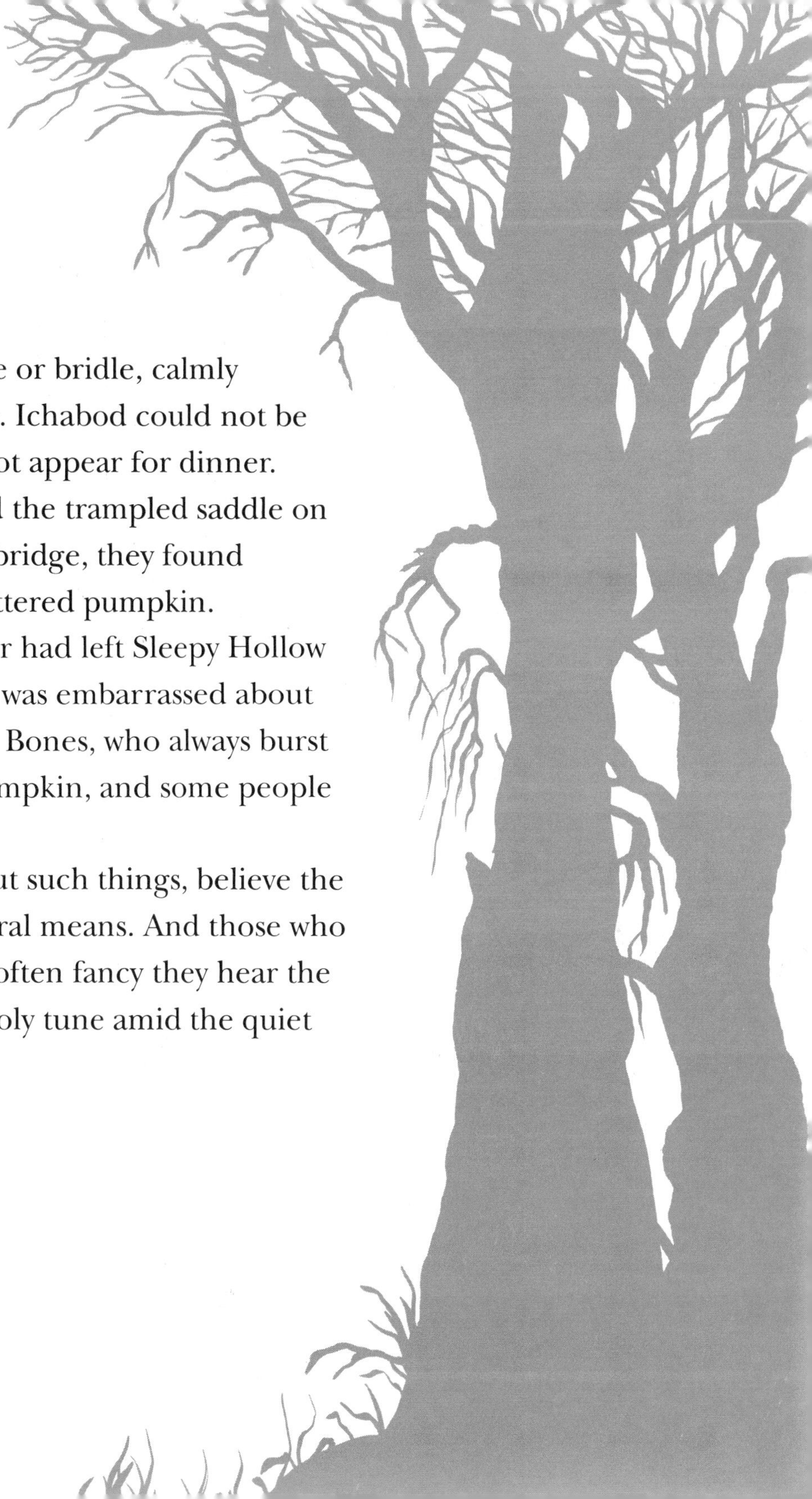

Washington Irving
(1783-1859)

Born in New York City, Washington Irving was the youngest of eleven children. As a boy, he explored much of the New York countryside which later served as a backdrop for his folktales.

By the time Irving was twenty-six, he was a well-established writer in both the states and in Europe, but he did not use his own name on his work until he was in his fifties. His many pseudonyms were Jonathan Oldstyle, Launcelot Wagstaffe, and Friar Antonio Agapida. *The Legend of Sleepy Hollow* first appeared in his collection of stories entitled *The Sketch Book of Geoffrey Crayon*.

He was the first American author to receive widespread critical acclaim abroad as well as at home, fulfilling his lifelong dream of creating American folklore. The sales of his popular stories brought him a handsome fortune.

Irving died in Tarry Town, and was posthumously elected to the American Hall of Fame in 1900.